Calling on a Bad Day

A Rescue Sisters Story

Karina Fabian

LASER COW PRESS

Laser Cow Press

Merritt Island, FL

Laser Cow Press
Merritt Island, FL
https://fabianspace.com

Publisher's Note: This is a work of fiction. Names, characters, places, and incidents are a product of the author's imagination. Locales and public names are sometimes used for atmospheric purposes. Any resemblance to actual people, living or dead, or to businesses, companies, events, institutions, or locales is completely coincidental.

Book Layout © 2017 BookDesignTemplates.com
Cover Art by Karina Fabian
Bible Quotes from the New American Bible, revised edition

Calling on a Bad Day/ Karina Fabian. — 1st ed.

Dedicated to anyone whose had a bad day at work. I feel ya!

For I know well the plans I have in mind for you...plans for your welfare and not for woe, so as to give you a future of hope.
Jeremiah 29:11.

"**B**less me Father for I have sinned. It's been four months since my last confession, six weeks since my last opportunity." Rae Marie Martingale paused for the expected comment.

The priest didn't congratulate her nor scold her for not grabbing every chance she got. Heaven knew they were few and far between in the asteroid belt. Instead, he acknowledged her statement with a nod.

They were tucked into a little alcove in the passenger waiting area of Waylaid Port, but people passed by without paying attention. No one paid much attention here, except to how they could get off that rock. People flowed around one another, eyes on tablets or on schedules on the walls, never noticing the other humans around them. Rae had been like them herself that day, but some instinct told her to look up just as she saw the priest looking over the list of ships heading out. She'd gone right up to him and asked him to hear her confession.

"Go on," he said calmly.

She made her confession, mostly petty thefts from one part of the company to pay to get some other thing in the company accomplished, and of course, entertaining thoughts of violence against her boss, her coworkers. Then she awaited her penance.

Instead, he asked, "Do you like your job?"

What did that have to do with anything? But she would neither lie to nor snark at a priest, especially in the middle of a sacrament, so she said. "I like flying. Flying here? Not so much. My next assignment, for example: *Lucky Charms*, the most run-down and abused ship on Waylaid—and that's saying a lot. Maybe I should have you come administer Last Rites. My boss is—well, you know." She'd confessed enough. "So, no, I can't say I do."

"Part of making a good confession is making a sincere effort to not sin again. Jesus said if your right hand causes you to sin, cut it off."

"You want me to cut off my hand?" That would certainly wreck her ability to pilot a spacecraft. But, really? What kind of priest was he?

He smiled with gentle amusement. "No. Of course not. But your job situation seems to put you in occasions of sin. As part of your penance, I want you to explore alternatives."

Now, she smiled, but not as sweetly. "This is Waylaid, Father. Not a lot of alternatives if you don't have the credits to relocate."

"Pray. Pray for guidance. Trust Him to lead you. And also pray three Hail Marys and an Our Father, slowly, really contemplating the line 'as we forgive those who trespass against us.'"

Afterward, she thanked him and received a blessing.

"One question," he said as he stood. "The 'opportunity' six weeks ago—was that another priest you happened to see in a port?"

She grinned sardonically. "Guilty as charged. He was talking to the dockmaster, so..."

"I see. Interesting." He left without explaining his statement.

Once he'd gone, she lingered to say her prayers.

Lord, You know how much I want out of here, she prayed. I mean, it's not like I haven't told You. But maybe I need to trust more. So here's the deal: I'm going to trust You to guide me. Just, show me the way to go.

She said "Amen" and headed to the dock to see what form her "daily bread" might take.

Turns out, God had a sense of humor.

I'm trusting. I'm trusting. I'm trusting.

Rae Marie Martingale stared out the observation window at the ship she'd been assigned. To say the Lockheed-Mac 397 had seen better days was like saying St. Lawrence got a sunburn. The hull of the *Lucky Charms* was scarred and pitted like someone had deliberately flown through a debris field—or created one by crashing the ship into some unfortunate rubble pile. She thought she saw a faint blue cloud near the port injectors. The transfer barge docked with it, and she could swear it listed. How did a ship list in the vacuum of space?

Laughter broke her thoughts.

"Second thoughts?" Gelt smirked. "If you're not up to it…"

Gelt was the company dockmaster on Way-laid, which wasn't nearly as auspicious a position as it was on a real station like Ceres. However, he made up for it with an abundance of tyranny and incompetence, coupled with a lasciviousness that shone in his piggy eyes. He couldn't do much to her as she was the best—and cheapest—pilot on the company payroll, thanks to her excess of skill and lack of formal education. She was saving every credit she could for flight school, just to get the certs that would get her off this rock permanently.

With Gelt handling her assignments, it was like flying against the sun both ways.

Maybe indentured servitude wouldn't be so bad... There were laws for the ethical treatment of ISs, plus a nice simple contract: X years commitment for room, board, and negotiated benefits, like flight school. Regular ol' employees, on the other hand...People figured if you're willing to take the pain for the pay, it was none of their business.

Pain. She glanced at *Lucky Charms*. A second blue cloud had joined the first.

Then, she had a sudden vision of Gelt buying her contract and shuddered.

He was waiting for her answer, his grin mocking.

"I can fly it," she snarled. *St. Gillian, pray for me!*

He shrugged. "Never said you couldn't." He made a show of looking at his tablet. "So... cargo: American turkeys, two gross, live."

"Live?" Rae squawked.

Gelt peered at her from under raised brows. "Some dirtsider on a luxury liner wants to treat passengers and crew to a genuine Christmas dinner. If he's got the plastic..."

"Does he? Then why are we transporting them in *Lucky*? Live animals aren't cheap—why risk losing them on the last leg of their journey?"

Gelt responded with a glare. "Are you intending to lose the cargo?"

"Of course not! But—" She flung her arm toward the bay window at the barely flight-worthy wreck. She thought she saw one of the rocket modules sag as if in agreement.

Gelt shrugged. It was his standard response to everything from "Where do you want to eat?" to "Was that a hull breech?"

"I don't ask those questions," he said, even though that was practically in his job description. "*Lucky Charms* needs to get to Ceres for an overhaul, and the turkeys need to get to Ceres for pickup by the *Stellar Opalescence*. Besides, I got you an engineer. Name's Chin. He's Chinese or maybe Japanese? Says 'Aso' a lot. Anyway, he'll keep things running as far as Ceres."

"Now, speaking of needs: You also have passengers. They need off station in a hurry."

Rae gaped. Turkeys were bad enough. They didn't know any better. But actual, living, *thinking* humans? "They asked for a ride in that?"

"I don't think they're especially picky." He jerked his head toward the airlock. A station security van pulled in, and a grim-faced officer stepped out. As the door opened, she heard several male voices chorusing about Mars needing women.

"You the pilot?" the officer demanded. Before she could decide how to answer, he handed her a tablet. The document remanded to her custody Toffleer, Doug; Adams, Stormy; Boon, Misha; Boon, Bud; and McGillicutty, Norman. Drunk and disorderly. Charges waived if they left the station within the hour.

"How disorderly?" Rae asked.

The van began rocking. The officer glanced at it and raised his brows at her.

"*Mars Needs Women/And So Do We!*" came the merry chorus from the van. The policeman's partner was trying to coax them out. Suddenly, one spilled out the door, embracing the startled policeman, and shouted, "I'm Doug! Ask me about my couplings!"

This could not be my way out of here. She handed the tablet back to the officer. "I'd rather swim in vacuum."

Gent snorted. "You need this job. Besides, I've got a bonus for you."

"Bonus?" There were few words as beautiful as the promise of extra credits. That much closer to flight school and respectability...

But Gelt swiped on his pad, then handed it to her. It was a photo of the priest who'd heard her confession. The curriculum vitae said he was Father Kyle St. James, roaming priest, currently assigned to the Order of Our Lady of the Rescue. Coincidence or divine sign?

"He's already onboard and waiting. Or I could get Blazer to fly," Gelt suggested.

There was no way she'd trust a priest to Blazer's flying. He was probably the one who got *Lucky Charms* was in such a state. "No. It's fine. I've got it."

"Thought you might like the chance to meet with an actual priest," he gloated. "You can confess all those terrible things you've thought about me."

"That could take the whole trip. But I want a D'n'D waiver. The company is not sticking me for damages caused by vaccing drunks."

"You need this job," he repeated.

"Not as much as you need a pilot. A real pilot. You really think Blaze will keep this hulk going past Rest Stop?"

As they stood there, eyes locked in a battle of wills, the half-to-mostly-drunk men in fezzes ran up to them, the officer trailing behind, resigned.

Their leader, a tall, stocky man with gold braid on his sleeves, leaned on his knees to catch his breath, then stood and looked at the three in turn. The top left of his shirt flashed between "Hi! My name is Doug!" and "Ask me about my couplings."

"We missed our ship. They said you're the only thing heading to Ceres in time. Who's the pilot? We'll pay double if you take us and our cargo!"

Rae grinned.

Two hours later, her victory didn't seem so sweet. Two of the businessmen (she used the term only because they insisted they'd been on their way to a trade show) had made passes at her. Doug had kept trying to put his chest in her line of sight while she got them settled into seats for the flight. Like she was going to ask him about his couplings. They were locked away in the old. That was all she needed to know. Then one of the Boons had thrown up on her. She'd thought it was Misha, but they were identical twins, and she was pretty certain they kept switching their names to mess with her. Or maybe they were too drunk to keep even themselves straight. Regardless, their name tags also switched, saying "Bud" one minute and "Misha" the next.

If Fr. Kyle hadn't been there, she might have been tempted to "accidentally" forget to set the air scrubbers for eight humans (plus the two-gross of turkeys). Who was she kidding? Her inebriated passengers probably would have enjoyed the experience. She left Father in the "private cabin"—really a broom closet with a porthole window and a seat—to say his prayers and headed to the bridge.

The Lock-Mack 397 was made for long-haul operations or short cargo runs like Rae specialized in. Thus, its bridge could accommodate three crewmen, but with the right workarounds, a single pilot could easily handle everything. For some reason, when *Lucky Charms* was retrofitted, they didn't remove the captain's chair with its minimal controls and overrides, nor did they tear out the comms/engineering panel, despite the fact that the controls connected to nothing, and the lights blipped and flashed in random patterns that served no purpose except to look impressive to paying passengers. Rae had no intention of impressing anyone on this flight, and the weak lights coming from the displays seemed to support that decision.

She took her seat at the pilot's console and said a quick prayer for a safe trip, for guidance in her life, and for the patience to not lock anyone in the spare cargo hold on the way.

Despite her devotion, when she'd cleared port, she'd gunned the engine in frustration and desire to get there fast. The *Lucky Charms*' alarms started wailing like she'd gone *kouritza* and had pointed them all toward Mars.

A squawk sounded beside her. The comms were out, but Gelt had provided walkie-talkies. Chin was calling from Engineering to complain. "What are you doing?"

He sounded young and frantic. She could hear alarms howling like rabid banshees around him.

"Sorry!" She eased off the thrusters. "I'll go more carefully."

"Please!"

Once they were cruising, she set the autopilot and looked over her controls. *Nominal. Nominal. Complaining. Not Right. Definitely Skewed. Why Are You Hurting Me So?* and *I'm Dying and Will Take You With Me!*

Eleven hours. Just hold it together for Eleven more hours. She wasn't sure if she was talking to the ship or herself.

She keyed the walkie talkie. "How are things going down there, Chief?"

"Chief?" Chin asked. The sirens in his section had stilled. Now, she could hear an odd clunking. *Thunkythunkyclunk.*

"You are my chief engineer, right?"

"Yes...?" *Thunkythunkyclunk.*

She chose to ignore the whimper in his voice. "We're at cruising speed. I've got a couple of urgent indicator lights. Can you check them?"

She started with the most important (which only claimed *Definitely Skewed*) and ended with the most urgent (*Death! Doom! Oh, Waily-waily!*).

"I'm not seeing any issues on this end," Chin said about the last one. *Thunkygriiiiind-clunkythunk.*

With a sigh, she thumped the display with the base of her fist. The needle jumped, then settled into a nervous, *Yeah, I'm Good. It's Good. We're Good. How Are You?*

"Did you...hit it?" Chin asked.

"Didn't they teach percussive maintenance in your fancy engineering school?" She was being sarcastic, but he replied with complete seriousness that he must have been hungover that day.

Ten and a half hours...

She instructed her chief engineer to remedy the alerts that he could and warn her if they were going to explode so she could make her last curses toward Gelt before getting Father Kyle to hear her confession. Then she unbuckled and went to check her cargo.

She took the long route to avoid the passengers. Maybe they'd finally passed out, and she would have a few hours' peace. A ghostly wisp of song through the vents chided her for dreaming too big. Instead, she turned her mind to the turkeys. She'd never seen live ones before. She'd never seen any turkey, other than a photo her uncle had shown her when he was teaching her about Earth. She'd never given it much thought—she'd been more interested in learning how to pilot their ship.

She got to the cargo hold. The gasket around the door was starting to crumble. She sighed and concentrated on the turkeys. There was a bag of grain beside the door. Was she expected to feed them? Gelt hadn't said, and it wasn't in the written orders for the haul. Would they eat out of her hand, like the station cat sometimes did? That would be sweet.

But no. That was not enough grain for the nearly 300 turkeys in the hold. Was it to keep them calm while she inspected them? It might be kind of interesting to walk among the cages, cooing at the birds, the turkeys delicately pecking seed out of her hands...

She opened the door and discovered several of the crates were busted, whether by the handlers or the huge birds, she could not tell. Dozens of turkeys wandered the room, gobbling and pecking at the wood. Some of the other crates were starting to splinter.

For a moment, she watched frozen, thinking only, *Wood? What greenfoot pays to use wood crates instead of composite plastics?*

Maybe she said something aloud. Suddenly, every gobbler in the room went silent, and scores of hate-filled eyes turned her way— which meant they were looking at her in profile, but somehow that made it all the more terrifying.

Then, as if understanding their eventual fate and the opportunity the open door provided, they charged.

"Gah!" She shoved the door shut. An indignant squawk and resistance told her she'd caught some tom's foot in the door. She loosened her pressure and kicked the leg. Another squawk and the leg retreated.

I probably crippled him, she thought, then dismissed the incident from her mind. A broken leg won't make him any less edible; besides, he'd probably had something even more dire in mind for her.

On the way back to the bridge, she heard her passengers calling:

"Oh, pretty captain!"

"Are we there yet?"

"For vac's sake! Again? How is your stomach not empty?"

She hurried to the bridge and closed the door—by hand; the autosliders were shot, of course. Then, she flopped into the mostly useless, but comfortable, captain's seat, determined to let the ship run on autopilot until the last possible second while she figured out how she'd sunk so low.

Naturally, someone had to knock.

She couldn't even get on the intercom to scare them off. That was broken, too,

The knocking continued, then changed cadence: *quickquick long quick. Quickquick long quick.*

Alleluia?

The cameras still worked. She turned on the one facing the other side of the door. Father Kyle was there, pounding desperately.

She undid the lock and pulled open the door partway. She heard Fr. Kyle: "Hurry!" and

Dave: "Hey, Father! Ask me about my couplings!" then the priest had slid through the narrow opening and slammed it shut. He leaned his back against the closed door, panting. He had a satchel across his body.

"When you asked me to give the ship Last Rites, I thought you were kidding!"

She gave him a sardonic grin. "Aren't you supposed to be out there ministering to the sinners?"

"I'll minister once they're sober," he promised. "Can I...use the bridge's head? The passenger ones are clogged."

Of course they were. She flopped back into the captain's chair. "Please, Father. Make yourself at home.

He set the satchel gently on the pilot's seat. A few minutes later, he emerged from the bathroom, looking somewhat more relaxed. "Thank you! I intended to stay quietly in my cabin and pray for their souls, but my lock's busted. And then—well, sometimes the call of nature can override even the most fervent spiritual intentions—not to mention the desire to remain unspotted from that particular world."

He jerked his chin toward the door with a sardonic grin.

"How are they still drunk?" Rae asked. "It's been hours!"

"Doug had a flask of 307 Ale hidden in his coupling prototype."

Rae moaned. 307 Ale: so named because it was supposed to be 153.5% alcohol, brewed in a tesseract to be the first hyper-beer. As far as she knew, that was so much bilge, but it was notorious for its extreme and lasting inebriation.

Ten more hours. St. Gillian, ride with us!

Father continued. "Apparently, their boss and, more importantly, *their wives*, are waiting for them on Ceres, so they intend to keep the party going as long as they can. Doug offered me a thimble. I did try to stop them. I tried to interest them in Mass, but none of them are Catholic."

She snorted and suggested, "They're probably Tequilatarian."

He laughed. "Bacchusists!"

"First Order Inebriapalians."

Father buckled over laughing. When he straightened, he wiped tears of mirth from his eyes and looked heavenward—or at least "up" since they were surrounded by the "heavens." "Lord, I apologize for my derogatory—if funny—thoughts."

Then he looked at her, amusement and pleading in his eyes. "May I stay here? I can sit and pray quietly if you prefer."

She felt a quiet stirring in her heart. "Actually, Father, it's been a long time—maybe we could hold a simple Mass?"

He smiled as if she'd given him a great gift. "Of course!"

"Hang on!" She got on the walkie-talkie. "Chin, you available?"

The thunking was continuing in the background, but he answered, "My name is Jaques."

For a moment, Rae's brain went offline, replaced by its own grinding of gears as she paradigm shifted to the new information. "*Jaques?*"

"I'm French Indonesian from Phobos." The engine seemed to complain along with him. *Thunkygriiind-thunkygriiind plupplurp.*

You left Phobos for Waylaid? What kind of idiot are you? But all she managed was, "Gelt said you were Chinese—or Japanese because you say 'Aso' a lot."

"That's not what I was saying," he replied quietly.

She paused to look at Father Kyle, who was biting back a grin.

"Okay, Jaques. Sorry. Anyway, are you Catholic? Because Father Kyle is on the bridge and said he'd do Mass for us if you can get away."

"Oui! Give me five minutes."

Thunkygriii—

WHAM!

Bluuurp! Thu-thu-thu-purrrr.

"Two minutes!" Jaques replied, triumph and surprise in his voice. "Wow. That worked."

"Take the Jeffries tube—the drunks are at the front door."

A sigh was his response.

The passengers were now standing (weaving) outside the bridge and serenading her with an off-key rendition of "Rocket Man." She knew it was the song because one of them was holding up a pad that scrolled the words. She guessed it was off-key based on how they sometimes snickered or pointed at one another, then jerked their finger up.

On the bridge, however, a kind of calm seemed to be settling as Father opened his satchel and took out his Mass kit. Or it should have. Rae had been to other "bridge Masses," so-called because they were held on the bridge of a ship doing short runs or who had one-deep crew positions. There was always something magical about the priest leading them through prayers, the stars from the viewscreen at his back, the quiet hums and muted beeps of the ship a background to the responses and songs.

But this was the *Lucky Charms*.

Father had just donned his stole when a banging came from the Jeffries tube, followed by a muffled "I'm stuck!"

The original door had been replaced by an oversized piece of metal screwed in at the four corners. The bottom one near the wall was stripped. The could only swing the door down about four inches, creating a little crack at the top. Jaques peeped through, but all he could see was the side wall opposite.

"We'll make do," Father Kyle said when the two apologized. "Kind of reminds me about the time I celebrated Mass with a group of Helium-3 miners trapped in a gas chamber on Eriadne's Folly. A malfunction caused the room to get flooded with gas. We had to wait three days for special equipment and a decontamination unit. They passed nutridrinks and air cannisters through a negative pressure vestibule we'd managed to create."

"Sounds terrifying!" Jaques said.

Father nodded, but there was something almost nostalgic in his eyes. "There was something...poignant...about being aware that any word might literally be your last. At least here, I can pass you the Host. We could only do the Eucharist with the wine on Eriadne's."

Father stepped back the makeshift altar and clasped his hands. "Shall we start? It's the Feast of St. Matthew, one of my favorites! In the name of the Father, and the Son, and the Holy—"

Squeee!

Rae leaped to the pilot's console and checked the alarms. A port thruster had fired. She slammed it shut. Then an indicator light flared red. "Jaques, I have a brownout of back-up power."

"I do, too. I'd better…"

While she corrected course, she heard him tap his tablet. "Hold on," he said. "It's gone now."

She checked her console. Yep, it now showed Nominal. "Huh. Stupid bucket of bolts! Sorry Father."

"No problem. Get a breath. Maybe we should start with the St. Michael prayer?"

St. Michael must have been busy that day. They managed a relatively calm Opening Prayers, but Rae still felt she like she was walking through the motions, reciting along with Father and Jaques while her eyes roamed from indicators to navigation control to the live feed of the raucous outside her door. Her passengers had given up singing and were trying to get at the camera.

Meanwhile, Father read St. Paul's exhortation to Ephesians. "I...urge you to live in a manner worthy of the call you have received, with all humility and gentleness, with patience."

She snorted, then winced, but Father went on undeterred.

Once upon a time, she'd understood gentleness and patience. Then, her uncle, who had raised her on his trading ship, died in an accident that destroyed their ship and their cargo. The insurance was enough to pay the damages and most of her medical bills, but when she left the hospital, she was alone, shipless, and broke. Sixteen was old enough in the 'Belt to be considered an adult, but not old enough to secure an apprenticeship with one of the big companies. She'd wandered, taking scut jobs and trying to save enough money to get her pilot's license, and ended up on Waylaid. But it seemed like every step forward was met with someone pushing her two back.

One of her fares—they'd now lost the privilege of being called "passengers" was licking the camera.

Patience? She'd used up her lifetime supply, and gentleness had evaporated even faster. Now, if humility meant enduring humiliation—that she continued to do in spades.

Whoever had been licking the camera must have been standing on someone's back. They toppled, and lay laughing. Meanwhile, the waste extraction had gone from green to amber. She clenched her fists against the urge to call up the levels and forced her mind back to the Mass.

As Father read about Jesus calling Matthew to be a disciple, she had to admit, she was a little jealous. I don't even know how to handle the idiots outside my door. *How nice it must be to have the Son of God go up to you and tell you exactly what you're meant to do.*

She blinked in surprise when Father said nearly the same thing in his homily.

"But we have to remember, we're looking at it with over two millennia of hindsight. We know how the story ends. But these men, they were being asked to leave what they knew—secure jobs, families, their plans for the future—to enter the unknown. If there's anything we should envy, it's their ability to trust so deeply..."

There it is again. Trust. I'm trying, God. Give me credit for trying?

Rae sighed and glanced at the viewscreen. Sometime between "Lead us not into temptation" and "I am not worthy that You should enter under my roof," their inebriated passengers had wandered off.

The waste extraction unit overpressured and blew during communion. The ship shook, and Father staggered just as he was placing Communion on Rae's tongue. His fist connected with her teeth.

"I'm fine!" he said shaking out his hand as alarms shrieked again. "Take care of the ship. Go in peace to love and serve the Lord!"

Fortunately, he'd given Jaques his first. The engineer was already heading back to engineering, but over the walkie talkie, he said, "What do I do first?"

"What do you—?" she started, but of course, the walkie talkie was off and she was using both hands to get the ship back on course and figure out what else was going on.

Father hesitantly reached for the walkie-talkie, she just jerked her head to indicate permission. He keyed it for her. The pause gave her time to check her temper. *Please just be that green and not a complete idiot!*

"The waste extractors blew and is shooting...crap...out the port quarter. Find the nearest valve and close it!"

"Nearest valve... Won't that make it back up in here?"

"It's knocking us off course. I have limited reaction fuel. Shut the valve and disable the flush option in the toilets."

"That's gross."

"Do it! Then figure out why backup power's out."

"What, again? Any idea what page in the manual covers toilets?"

"*What?*"

"Never mind!" Jaques' reply ended with a squawk and static.

Rae swore, then apologized. "I know I should feel more peaceful, especially after the Eucharist, but—"

"Just breathe. You know Jesus came to Peter and the other disciples after they'd had a long night of not catching fish. Who knows? He might have Called Matthew on a bad day, too."

"So there's hope?" she asked sardonically.

He replied with irritating peace: "Faith, hope, and love."

A moment later, the ship steadied. Either Jaques had found the page or the current supply of biowaste had run out. Either was fine by Rae.

Father set the walkie-talkie down. "Maybe I should go check on the others? At very least tell them to 'hold it' until we get to Ceres. Any idea where they are?"

Rae pointed to the control for the different cameras and let him flip through views while she assessed the situation. Fuel down: 40%. Toilets disabled—or would be. Backup power...still out. All of it. How does that happen?

At least air and heat were fine. And the cargo—

"Uh-oh!" Father called.

Their passengers were crowding the cargo room door, watching as one of the Boons—the one that had not thrown up—picked the lock, if that's what you could call what he was doing. He was alternatively jiggling something in the keyhole and yanking at the handle. With each hard yank, she saw a tiny snowfall of disintegrating rubber shower their heads.

They didn't seem to notice. She could tell they were giggling. A couple were grabbing handfuls of grain from the bag by the door.

"The turkeys! They think they're going to feed the turkeys! No! No." She jammed her finger on the intercom button and yelled for them to stop, her voice getting louder the more they didn't hear her.

The door had opened, and two dozen space-crazed specimens of *meleagris gallopavo domesticus* stampeded into the hallway. Forgetting the *domesticus* in their species designation, they trampled over Bud Boon like he was a welcome mat. Or was it Misha? One flew up at Misha (or maybe Bud), who ran scream-ing like a girl. At least Rae assumed that's how he sounded. He was waving his hands around his head like a girl in an old Earth horror flick trying to protect her hair from bats. The tur-key, well-fattened for the dinner table, was only able to fly up a few feet, but that was enough to hook its toes around Boon's belt. It managed to peck him in the shoulder blades a time or two, but when it reared back for the kill, it overbalanced and flopped back, taking Boon with it. Rae could almost hear the squish.

"My cargo!"

Boons One and Two were on the ground, moaning. Doug was cowering behind the door with the feed grain. Stormy was buckled over laughing. That left Norman, who chose the better part of valor and ran. As one, the tur-keys raced after him. Perhaps it was the grain in his pockets. Or maybe the turkeys simply responded to fear. Hadn't her uncle said some-thing about birds being descended from prehistoric predators?

She vowed to never set foot on Earth.

In the meantime, she had to get control of her cargo!

Unable to see the havoc on the screen, Jaques had already backed down the Jeffries tube and presumably was heading to the chaos.

She grabbed her walkie-talkie, then froze. What should she do? There was nothing in the manual for when angry, deranged livestock broke containment and swarmed the ship like some kind of invading—

That's it!

She ran back to the captain's chair. One of the seldom-used protocols that was still attached to its control was the ability to lower blast doors. She didn't know why they called them blast doors—no blasting was involved. They were meant to seal off any part of the ship that might have a leak. However, the captain had the ability to override the controls and manually shut them. Maybe she could restrict the turkeys' movement until they could figure out how to corral them back into the cargo hold. The passengers would get stuck, but they could lead them out through the Jeffries tubes.

Once they sobered up.

And signed a confession saying the Great Turkey Exodus was their fault.

And gave her the rest of their ale.

She pulled up a schematic of the ship, focusing on the cargo bay outward. "How fast can turkeys move?"

"Are you asking me?" Father asked.

It had been rhetorical, but she fired back, "Got a guess? Divinely inspired preferred."

Meanwhile, she started with some of the doors nearest the chaos. She only needed four to close off the area... Three...

The next one bounced with an alert: *Obstacle detected. Continue? Y/N*

Was it a turkey? Junk that rolled in the way? Was Norman passed out across the threshold? She couldn't find a camera to show her, so she rejected the override. She could always close the next door down.

But when she tried to lower the next door, she found her rejection had been applied to all the doors.

"That's not how it's supposed to work!" she yelled at the chair, which simply replied with an obstinate, *Command denied. Please enter override code.*

She typed in her code.

Code rejected. Please enter Captain's level code.

"I am the captain! And the pilot. And apparently now a turkey wrangler!" she shouted. Strangely enough, the ship's computer had no response for her outburst.

She went to the storage closet. "Think stunning the turkeys will change how they taste?"

Again, Father said, "I have no idea. I'm from the Rings."

"I'll chance it. Do you have any compunctions against shooting a bird? I promise, they are not innocent," she said as she punched her code into the weapon's locker. It worked there, at least.

But the locker was empty.

"What?" she cried. The weapons locker was for defending the ship against pirate attacks. Had the company not trusted her to not shoot her passengers or had they decided the ship was not worth defending? "Now what?"

"Do you have a first aid kit at least?" Father asked. "Misha—or maybe Bud—is bleeding, and I'll bet those turkey claws aren't sanitary."

"Right. People first. But here." She handed him a broom with the first aid kit. "Just in case."

"Good thinking." Father stuffed the kit into his satchel as best he could and grabbed the broom like a quarterstaff.

She took the mop for herself.

They passed the "obstructed" hatch that had refused to close and had shut down the rest in solidarity. There was vomit on the tracks. It was chunky. Rae prayed for self-control because patience seemed like too big an ask, and they moved on.

At least they made it to the cargo hold without encountering a crazed clucker. She was just about to count her blessing when she saw that her infuriating fares had dragged their friend into a seated position and were trying to pour alcohol down his throat.

"Give me that!" She grabbed the flask and the cap that Doug was holding to Misha's?—Bud's? —*Boon's*—lips. A little of the ale spilled onto Boon's chest, and he shrieked as the alcohol seared the wound.

"It's for the pain!" Dough protested as Boon's cries turned to whimpers. Father knelt down, opened the kit, and started tending his wounds.

"There would have been a lot less pain if you hadn't been drinking in the first place!" she retorted. "Father, you okay there?"

Father Kyle was wrapping Boon's hand while directing Stormy, Norman, to dab disinfectant on the scratches on Boon's face. "Yeah. They look mostly superficial."

She crossed over to the other Boon, who was still lying on his back, which arched weirdly because of the turkey under him.

"You okay?"

"I think so?"

She paused, expecting more. Finally, she asked, "So why haven't you gotten up?"

"I'm afraid?"

The tom he had squashed was unconscious, but twitching. Did that mean it was waking up or in its death throes? She put the mop over its face, then knelt by its neck. Directing Doug to help pull Boon up and Norman to get ready to hold down the bird's body, she set her hand on its neck. She could feel the blood pumping. "It's still alive. Get ready. Okay—now!"

Doug yanked Boon up and forward. Boon collapsed into Doug's arms. Norman, meanwhile, threw himself on the turkey like a courageous soldier might throw himself on a grenade. The turkey heaved once, then decided to give up, save for gobbling promises of fowl revenge.

Carefully, she removed the mop. Its round eye was blacker than space, yet, she got the impression that it was hurting—and it expected her to do something about it.

She stretched out her leg. "Father, get the dropper out of the first aid kit and the flask out of my pocket and give me about point-five CCs of ale."

"Hey, don't waste it!" Doug protested.

"You want to take it up with the bird?" She loosened her grip slightly. The tom bucked.

Doug backed up, his hands in surrender.

The turkey watched with interest as Father filled the dropper. Whether it understood or was simply fascinated by the shiny surface of the flask, she didn't know, but it did accept their offering. She watched as it swallowed, the muscles in its neck constricting. Then, it gave a great shudder and relaxed.

"I need a rope or a belt of something."

Soon, she had it leashed. It stood, wobbling and gobbling to itself. It followed her docilely into the second cargo hold, and she left it leaning against a wall. It made a warbling purring sound. She hoped that was a good sign.

"There's one," she said.

"So now what? Get them all drunk?" Stormy asked.

He was joking, but it wasn't that bad an idea. If only there were a way without force-feeding a volatile alcohol into an equally volatile bird. Then she noticed the torn and spilling seed bag by the door.

"How about the feed?" Rae said. "We could soak some in the ale."

Doug groaned. "Not my ale! That's all I have left!"

"What about the one in your—" Stormy started and was hushed, but not quickly enough. Soon, Rae had another, nearly full, flask and the reassurance that the party was indeed over.

Doug continued to grumble. "Three-oh-seven's not cheap, you know!"

It was a testimony to the effect Mass had had on her that she didn't take his head off and use it as bait for the turkeys. "Tell the company to take it out of any damage done by those birds you and your friends released."

Doug muttered, "How could they tell?"

Rae looked around the already battered and well-worn hallway. He had a point. However, that reminded her of something else.

"Has anyone seen Jaques?"

"Who?"

"Jaques. My chief engineer. French Indonesian Phobosian? Kind of a deer-in-the-headlights look?" That was the extent of her ability to describe him.

Without waiting for their answers—which, really, was a series of shrugs, anyway—she got on the walkie-talkie. "Chief, where are you?"

"Jeffries tubes?" came the hesitant reply.

"Okay... Where in the Jeffries tubes?"

"I…don't know." He sounded defeated.

"Are you lost?" She pressed the walkie-talkie against her forehead, said a prayer for strength, then spoke again. "Look. There should be a map of the ship on your tablet—"

"That's just it. I don't have it. The turkey does."

"The…"

"Turkey. I exited the tube just past the cargo bay, starboard, and this guy ran screaming past me, a dozen of them on his tail. They're huge! Anyway, one saw me, and I just, I dunno, panicked! I swung the tablet at him."

"Then you dropped it?"

"No! The turkey pecked it out of my hand. It's like a ninja turkey! Anyway, bunch of them just, descended on it, pecking and scratching. I ducked back into the Jeffries tube and by the time I slowed down, I realized I didn't know which way I'd gone!"

She did not have time for this. If the turkeys had gone down the starboard corridor, they'd come to one of the blast doors—which meant Norman McGillicutty was going to be cornered. Imagined screams and primal, gurgling howls playing in her mind, she told Jaques, "Find a junction. There are small arrows to show port, starboard, fore, and aft. Use them to find your way back to Engineering. Starboard aft."

"That's what those are! See? I'm learning so much!"

She didn't bother to reply, although she had this insane thought that he expected a cookie and to be told he was a good boy.

"How is he your chief engineer?" Stormy asked.

"Shut up and grab a bucket from that closet," she said.

Minutes later, they were heading down the hall, she in front, with a bucket of ale-soaked grain, the others crowding behind her, each holding some kind of long-handled cleaning implement at the ready. Already, they were hearing the growing din of gobblers: excited yelps interspersed with a metallic thunking—but no screams.

"Is he unconscious?" Father Kyle wondered worriedly.

As they neared the last blind curve before the blast door, Jaques contacted her. She paused to take his call.

"Hey, I found a guy in the tubes."

"McGillicutty?"

"That's what his name tag says. He's kind of scratched up and blubbering." He apparently held the keyed walkie-talkie to the man because they heard someone mutter. "Those eyes! The beaks. What is that….thing!...on their beaks?"

"What do you want me to do?" Jaques asked.

"Sounds like shock more than anything, and he's probably just sobering up. If he can stand, take him with you to Engineering. We're going to wrangle the turkeys."

"Roger that."

She turned to the others. "If we go in a group, we might scare them." *I know we'd scare me.* "Hang back here. Be ready to rush in if I scream. Otherwise, we'll wait until the feed relaxes them and see if we can calmly herd them to the cargo hold."

She made sure each of them gave her a nod, then she took a deep breath and started forward, bucket in front of her. "Here, turkey-turkeys," she called gently, falling into an ages-old rhythm that came from millennia of humans trying to fool animals into thinking they were best friends who had no ulterior motives.

From the way the gobbling died down to silence and heads jerked right then left, she wasn't sure they were buying it. But at least they weren't attacking.

"Look, guys! I brought a treat." Carefully, she reached into the bucket and pulled out the damp and sticky seed mush and tossed some in front of her. The turkeys in the front flapped their wings in surprise, then pounced on the grain hungrily.

"Good boys. Come on, now, don't be greedy..." She threw more in front of her, backing up slowly. "We're coming! Fall back," she called behind her as she continued to step back, tossing some feed to the back so that the ones furthest away got a little taste, too.

One of the toms got greedy and rushed her.

"No!" she yelped, kicking out reflexively. The heavy sole of her mag boot connected with its chest, and it dropped back. Whether the ale was taking effect or they had finally recognized her dominance, the rest followed without aggression.

They were going to run out of feed soon, but the toms continued to eat greedily. "Hey, guys. Get the feed and make a trail leading into the cargo hatch and toss the bag in! And two of you block the other corridor," she called.

She'd just run out of grain when Father showed up with a stash gathered in his shirt. The turkeys were starting to stagger a bit and were emitting a king of amused cooing. The ones to the back were more sober, but seemed willing to take the lead, especially with the promise of more grain.

Rae took a handful out of Father's stash and tossed it to the ones in the back. "Keep leading them," she told him. "I'll let them move past me and make sure there aren't any stragglers."

"Be careful," he said, and dropped some seed in front of him. The turkeys in the front tasted, paused, and looked at him suspiciously, like he'd gotten their order wrong. Then, with avian shrugs, they accepted the drier grain. Rae followed along behind, ready to swing the bucket at any turkey that decided it wasn't interested in a meal, but apparently, they'd decided they'd had enough excitement.

By the time they got to the door, they were so focused on the trail that they didn't even notice crossing the threshold. A few noticed the bag of grain and, with a happy yelping sound, dashed to it. The others quickly followed.

Yes! Come on, come on. Just a few more...

The first turkey, now apparently past the inebriation and into the hangover, let out a series of loud, sharp notes. The turkeys all stopped and raised their heads in alarm.

Shoot. "Go, go go!" Rae used the bucket to try to herd them in, just as the others were starting to realize that they might prefer to be out. The moment of indecision between food and freedom was not long enough.

They charged.

"Shut it!" Father shouted, pulling Rae out of the way. Doug, who had been standing ready, shoved with all his might.

With the gasket, the door did not slam, but made a kind of sucking sound, as it closed tight.

Leaving three confused, betrayed fowls on the wrong side.

Making hollow putt-putt-putts in alarm, the hens cowered behind the tom.

The tom ruffled its feathers. Its face grew fiercely red. It lowered its head in the direction of the two men trying to block the passageway.

"Stand fast, men," Doug said.

The tom charged.

Squealing in a way that would probably embarrass their wives, the two hugged the walls. The tom, more interested in freedom than avenging its imprisoned comrades, dashed down the corridor, followed by the two hens.

"No!" Rae leaped forward, swinging her bucket in an arc. She hoped to capture one of the hens, but her boot landed on some turkey poo. She slid and fell flat on her face. The bucket grazed its tail feathers, and the hen jumped startled, and pooped some more.

"Dang it!" she shouted.

"Easy!" Father Kyle said, helping her up. "Like the Rescue Sisters say, 'Faith, Hope, and Love.' We got most of them, right? Let's have a little faith."

That's when the power went out.

Someone—Doug, she thought—screamed. Even Father let out a surprised, "Whoa!"

What Rae wanted to shout was somewhat more obscene. Instead, she repeated, "Jesus, I trust in You," three times and told Father there should be a head lamp in the med kit. Meanwhile, everyone activated the lights in their wristcomps.

She grabbed her walkie-talkie from her pants pocket.

"Chief, please tell me you're in Engineering."

"Why are the lights out?" came the reply. In the background, she heard McGillicutty whimpering, "It was them! They're evil, I tell you."

What she wasn't hearing were the air recyclers.

"The main engines have died, Chief. You need to get backups running and figure out how to fix the main drive."

"Without lights? How much vacleak are we in? I don't hear the scrubbers! Are we going to *die*?" Her engineer's voice rose to a panicked pitch while in the background, his charge was in a panic all his own: *The turkeys! It was the turkeys. They've doomed us all.*

Faith, hope and love. Faith, hope, and love… "Norman," she adjusted her cadence as if comforting a child, "the turkeys are locked up now, okay? They can't hurt you. Jaques, it's a big ship. We have probably two days of breathable air. We have maybe half a day before the cold gets us."

"Twelve hours before we *freeze to death?*"

"*Twelve hours* to get the ship functioning," she retorted. "Are you in Engineering?"

"Almost? I thought I saw the vent I left open, but then the lights went out.

"Do you have the light in your wristcomp on?"

A pause, then, "Oh, yeah!"

She bit back a sigh. *Take the win.* "Good. Get to Engineering. Auxiliary controls are the port-aft module. Get the backup generator running."

"Hang on. I think I see the problem back here."

In the tubes? And I thought he didn't have any training. "Okay. Talk to me. Describe what you see."

Instead, he said, "Hang on."

A moment later, the corridor filled with light, and after a couple of coughs, the air recycling system started to purr. The passengers around her cheered.

Maybe he was an engineer, after all! "Wow! Well done, Chief. What was the problem?"

"It was unplugged. I guess that's what I snagged my foot on when I was heading to Mass."

Father Kyle set a hand on her shoulder. "Just breathe," he instructed.

"Faith, hope, and love," she muttered like a mantra.

While Jaques got his stray settled in a corner of Engineering and made notes of the many alarm indicators now indicating alarm, and the sober-and-fully-cowed passengers agreed to wait quietly in the passenger area, Rae and Father headed back to the bridge.

"There should be another tablet with a manual on the bridge," Rae said. "If you can take it and assist?"

"No problem. I have some engineering experience, myself. Small craft, but I'll do what I can."

As they came to the first turn, however, they were confronted with the escaped tom. It spread its wings, fluffed its feathers to twice its natural size, and lowered its red-faced head. Rae tried roaring back at it, her arms outstretched in her own imitation of wings, but this was a tom on the edge. It had seen its friends horribly betrayed by the Foodbringers. One of its friends had been squashed. Now it had two hens to protect and it wasn't taking any crap.

It charged.

Rae and Father were halfway down the wrong corridor when they realized it had stopped its advance and returned to the hens, which were yelping their approval. Their *ow-powpowps* cutting *cukcukcuks* echoed in the corridor.

"It's not worth it," Rae said to Father. "We can go around."

And thus it was that they were near the cargo airlock when another ship docked with them. It didn't do a very professional job of it, either; the bump nearly knocked the two off their feet despite the artificial gravity, and the clunk spoke of even more damage to be repaired on Ceres.

Rae immediately grabbed Father by the arm and pulled him into a corner. "We didn't send out a distress call. That's not rescue." Despite the noise of the airlock engaging, she spoke in a whisper as she backed them away.

"Certainly not an OLR vehicle," he whispered back. "No Rescue Sister would get certified with a sloppy execution like that."

"Pirates?" she speculated. *Sure, why not? I'm trusting You, God. I'm trusting.* "Father, can you get back to the passenger area? Get eve-ryone into the Jeffries tubes and head bridgeward."

"What are you going to do?" he asked.

"Stall. Here." She tapped on her wristcomp and swiped toward him. His own wristcomp beeped. "That's my commID. Text me when you are safe. Oh, and make sure everyone's comms are on silent! Go!"

The handwheel on the hatch was starting to turn. She stuck her mop handle in it and pulled in the opposite direction. She hissed at Father when he hesitated, and finally, he ran. Unwill-ing to let her sacrifice be in vain, apparently. Good.

If only there was some way to brace the handle against something to stop it from mov-ing, but no jutting metal presented itself. After a moment of jerking stops and starts, the wheel stopped trying to move. She didn't take that for granted; the person on the other end must be getting help. Still, with one arm draped over the pole so she could put her whole weight behind it, she used the other to contact Jaques.

"Lock up Engineering now. We've got pirates."

Static.

"Jaques!" she hissed.

Just then the wheel started to turn, and even her full weight was not enough. The mop handle bent, and she slid. She landed on her rump as the wheel started spinning and was just scrambling to her feet when the door flung open to reveal four men. Their hair was long and wild, and they had bearded chins. They wore loose shirts over their skinsuits and their pants bloused over their boots.

Funny, they didn't look like any pirates she'd ever seen.

For a moment, pirates and pilot stared at each other in surprise. Then one pirate broke the silence. "What are you doing here?"

"You're one to ask!" she retorted, standing up and dusting off her behind. She pulled herself tall. "I'm pilot and captain of *Lucky Charms*, Registry WL2893, under protection of Waylaid Transport and Shipping—"

Someone snickered, whether at her bravado or at the fact that she thought anything to do with Waylaid would strike fear. She continued, nonetheless. "You have secured an airlock and docked to my ship without permission. Present your authorization or leave immediately."

Now, they all snickered.

"Look, I have had a really bad day—"

The tall pirate in the back pulled out a weapon. "You stop talking now."

"Yep!" She threw her hands up in surrender. She'd never seen a gun so sleek. The single round hole in the end seemed to draw her gaze like a black hole.

"Where's the cargo?" the shorter, dumpier one asked. He looked like the most intelligent one of the group and also the least piratey.

But the guy with the gun had told her to stop talking, so she shrugged helplessly.

"You can talk!" he said, annoyed.

She glanced at the tall one. He shrugged laconically.

"What cargo?" she asked. "I'm taking this death trap to Ceres for a complete overhaul— or a mercy killing. The jury's out."

"Don't play smart—"

"I don't have to pretend—"

He stomped up to her. He was the same height as her and she realized his *mag* boots *weren't*. They were regular stationsider shoes. He poked her in the chest and shouted. "You have cargo and you have passengers. Take us to them or we start shooting!"

"The cargo or passengers?" she asked.

"We want the cargo live," one of the others chimed in.

"Then how do I know you won't take the cargo and shoot us before you leave?" she asked.

"Listen, Lady—"

"Captain," she corrected and watched his face grow a shade of red she'd only seen on turkeys. Regardless, she couldn't stall much longer. Either he'd have a coronary or they'd decide to shoot her for their own mental health and search the ship themselves.

Nonetheless, he started again. "Listen, Captain. I don't want your wreck of a ship. I don't even want your passengers. I do want your cargo. Now, take us to them like a good little girl, and we might just leave you alone to nurse this bucket of bolts to Ceres. Otherwise, we'll shoot you and anyone else who gets in our way. Copy?"

"Copy." She couldn't think of any other way to stall that wouldn't get her killed. The best she could do was take the long way and hope they didn't notice. Hopefully, she'd bought Father and the passengers to hide.

Hey, maybe we'll run into Turkey DonJuan and he'll take care of them, she thought. Then she had the start of an idea.

"This is the second time you've taken us down a level and back up," the lead pirate complained. "What are you playing at?"

"You said it yourself—this is a wreck of a ship. That last section isn't habitable. I had to lock it down with the blast doors."

"And this time?"

"Malfunction in the waste extraction unit—and drunk passengers. I evacuated them, but if you want to..?" It wasn't really a lie, just a mis-placement of legit information and an invitation for him to draw his own conclusions. Was it her fault he didn't ask for details?

He grunted and jerked his head for her to proceed down the ladder.

Still, she'd taxed his patience enough. "Down this corridor to the next ladder and then we're almost there," she promised.

When, at last, they reached the cargo area, she saw him cast a glance at one of the other pirates, who gave a small nod. However, when she led them to the hold with the loose turkeys, the subordinate cleared his throat.

"Don't get cute, Captain. Aren't they in there?"

He pointed to the original hold.

She gritted her teeth and let every ounce of frustration she'd felt on the trip slip through. "Yes! Yes, they were. But look!"

She stomped up to the door and ran a finger over the gasket seal. It disintegrated at her touch. The door moved slightly, its lock having been broken. She showed her dirty finger to him. "You think I was trusting the cargo to that seal? So I moved them."

"Really?" he sneered.

"Look around you," she said, indicating the room with its stray feathers, poop, and occasional blood stains. Then she pointed to her own excrement-smeared uniform, and finally to the other hatch. "Those cluckers have been a thorn in my side since I left port. They are now in there!"

One of the pirates swore sympathetically and with a hint of admiration at what he assumed was her Herculean effort at dragging two dozen crates of turkeys from one hold to the other.

"Fine," the leader said. "Show me."

She indicated for them to stand in front of the door, and for a wonder, they all did, crowding together nice and neat as she did the lock code and pulled open the hatch, keeping it between her and the pirates and the expected stampede.

Instead of the thunderous, gobbling mob she'd expected, there was...nothing.

Had she killed them with the grain?

"What the..?" The pirate leader stepped forward.

She peeked around the door. The turkeys were wobbling and clucking to themselves in a cross between alcoholic haze and food coma.

"About that…"

Suddenly, the other hatch door crashed open, and with a roar, Father Kyle and her passengers came screaming out and rushed the pirates.

The one with the gun shot.

Ping! Ping! Thwack!

The pirate leader screamed as the bullet lodged itself in his behind. He fell to the floor, squirming and howling.

As long as he had turned the other cheek, Rae took the opportunity to kick him into the cargo hold.

Meanwhile, her passengers and Father were grappling with the other pirates and shoving them into the hold as well.

One tripped over a hen, who let out a distressed yelp. Dozens of toms jerked to attention, and like any drunk alpha male seeing a female in peril, they were suddenly spoiling for a fight.

They managed to shut the door before pirate or turkey could escape.

She wanted to sit against the wall and bury her head in her hands, but her passengers were chest-bumping and high-fiving each other. From the open hold, the turkey had picked up on the commotion and were yelping and *owping* excitedly.

"I got a wristcomp!" Stormy cheered.

"I got the gun!" Misha crowed.

"Give me that!" The last thing they needed was for a still-intoxicated civilian to go shooting victory rounds in a ship. Who brings a projectile weapon on a ship, anyway?

She snatched the weapon from his hands, then stared at it, realizing she had no idea what to do with it. She'd never seen anything like this before.

Calmly, Misha took it back. He pressed a button to eject the magazine, then grabbed the top and pulled. She heard a *crrach-chik* and he declared the weapon clear.

"Four years' Army Infantry, Earth. *Hooah*!"

"How many more are there?" Bud asked. Maybe he was prior military, too.

"This is all that came on board," Rae said. She pulled out the walkie-talkie and tried Jaques again. No response. Dang it! Why hadn't she gotten his commID first thing?

"We have to check Engineering," Father said quietly. "The pirates might be there."

"He was already not answering when they were still attaching the airlock," Rae reminded him. "Maybe he saw them, and he and Norm are hiding?" Would it be too much to hope that there were pirates in Engineering, and they were actually fixing the ship? She'd be willing to leave them alone if so, at least until they took care of the rest.

"That's cold!" Bud said, and she realized she'd voiced her thoughts aloud. As she sputtered an explanation, he held up his hand. "No. I like it."

Meanwhile, Stormy was playing with the wristcomp. "This is a burner. There's only seven numbers on it. Think that's all of them?"

"Then that leaves three to go," Misha said. "Easy as pie. You got any weapons?"

She blinked. Not more than an hour ago, this guy was licking her camera lens. Now he was all commando? Still, she said, "If I did, do you think I would have gone after the turkeys with a bucket and a broomstick?"

"Why bother with a confrontation?" Father asked. "Let's just blast the airlock and separate the ships?"

"That won't do any good," Rae said. "We're dead in the Black, remember? They could reattach or worse, shoot at us."

Misha nodded. "Then we need a distraction."

And their eyes went to the open hold.

$\mathcal{R}$

"I hope this is a good idea," Rae whispered as she, Father, and Bud huddled to the side of the airlock. They'd left Doug to watch the holds. Misha and Stormy were hauling a crate of aggravated turkeys to the pirate ship.

"Faith, hope, and love," Father repeated the mantra of the Rescue Sisters. But he also crossed himself and held his hands in prayer as they listened over her open wristcomp as the hatch to the other ship opened.

"What the—where're my buddies?" The guard asked. He had a distinctly Ceres accent.

"Supervising the transfer," Misha grunted, seeming to strain with the load they were carrying. Then a *thunk* and a quick gobbling roar of protest as they set it down. "Where do you want this?"

"They sent you—alone?"

"They have a gun to the captain's head!" Stormy burst out. "She's a woman. Damn good looking, too. I don't want to see her brains on the deck."

The other man swore, as if surprised by his companion's viciousness. "Lars said he'd—? Hey! What's going on! What are you—?" His protest ended in a scream and a howl of fowl fury as Misha and Stormy, as planned, opened the case to release the turkeys.

"Run! Run!" Misha shouted, and apparently the man did because a moment later, he shouted, "Incoming!"

The pirate ran straight into Bud's out-stretched arm. He flipped and landed on his back. A dozen space-crazed turkeys trampled him on their blind and misguided quest for freedom.

"And then, there were two." Bud smirked up at Rae as he used the ties she'd found to bind their prisoner. The plastic ties were meant to hold equipment together when welding wasn't available; it would take special cutters to break those bonds.

"Two?" their prisoner said, "What happened to—Oh, vac! Who got away?"

Bud shoved a rag into his mouth and tied it. "Who got away?" he mused. Then he called Misha. "Looks like only one left, Mish."

"The pilot?" Misha replied. "No problem. He's surrendered."

"That's it?" Rae said. "It's over?"

"Kind of anticlimactic," Bud said.

Just as Father and Rae turned to gape at him, the gravity went out.

As soon as Rae felt her feet start to lift, she tapped a command on her wristcomp and her mag boots activated, sticking her to the floor. Only her hair, long escaped from its ponytail, floated freely.

The others weren't so lucky. Father, used to working in emergency situations, oriented quickly, but Bud started to panic and flail. His prisoner took that opportunity to push off a wall. He rocketed past them before Bud could get his bearings enough to grab him.

"Let him go," Rae said. He was heading down the same path as the turkeys. Soon enough, he'd probably run right into a cloud of bedraggled gobblers who had no idea how to handle zero g and would be plenty peeved about it. Sure enough, a moment later, they heard a bloodcurdling scream.

Doug was also screaming on her wristcomp. "What happened? What happened?"

Meanwhile, her walkie-talkie finally squawked. "Sorry! My bad."

"Jaques!" She didn't know whether to cheer with relief or chew him out for another snafu. "What happened? We couldn't get a hold of you. Did a pirate—"

"What pirate? We've got *pirates*?" She could almost hear him hyperventilate.

"Had. They're taken care of."

"They're what? Bilge in the Black, Captain! Is there anything you can't do?"

She clenched her fists, recited the Rescue Sister's mantra, and replied with forced calm. "Chief, why don't we have gravity? Better question: Are you in Engineering and can fix it?"

"Oh, no! We had to bug out. There was a turkey, see?"

"A turkey?"

"Well, yeah—a boy and a girl. I know because they were… Anyway. When he heard us, he came right at us, and we just ran and uh, got lost again—"

"Chief!"

"No, it's good! Otherwise, we'd have never seen the bomb."

"The what?"

"Yeah! And it was set to go off in like 45 minutes or if someone sent a signal. I mean, we're guessing. There was a wristcomp attached to it and it was counting down from 45, though that was like 20 minutes ago…"

"We have 25 minutes?" They had to abandon ship, get to the pirate ship and hope they got away in time to avoid the debris—

"What? No. Stand down, Captain. I disarmed it."

If it hadn't been for zero g, she'd have sunk to the ground. "You…*disabled* it?"

"Well, Norm and I did. He's got a mining op so he's seen explosives, and it really wasn't that complex a mechanism. Anyway, we thought it'd be best if we chucked it out the airlock, just to be safe, you know? Only, when I was taking it out, I bumped into the Hawkings stability compensator manifold, which, as you know, dictates the direction of the artificial gravity, so I panicked and just shut it all down. That was easy—there's a big red emergency button!"

She tapped the walkie-talkie against her head a few times. Above her, Father said, "Breathe. Just breathe."

There was no way they were repairing *Lucky Charms* at this point, not even enough to limp to Ceres. If her passengers could make it another seven hours. Bud was turning green and his cheeks puffed in a dangerous way. She pointed at him to Father, who took the hint and went to help him, or at least move him out of the way before he spewed.

Misha called then, "We're secure here. Shall we head back?"

"No," she said, an idea forming. "We're abandoning ship. We'll be bringing everyone to you."

"What about the *Lucky Charms*?"

She was half tempted to ask Jaques if he could reactivate the bomb, but of course, she couldn't. They had to keep the pirates locked up somewhere. Not to mention the turkeys. And the Company would charge her for damages, anyway, she was sure. No, it had to go with them.

"Hang on one." With a sigh, she got on the wristcomp to Doug. "I can't believe I'm saying this, but Doug, tell me about your couplings."

Who would have thought that the hour she spent in EVA with a priest who also knew how to handle a vac-welder would be the most peaceful part of her trip. As the two worked together to install Doug's couplings to hold the ships together, they talked about some of the crazy missions he'd been on.

"Though rampaging turkeys and pirates beats them all." He chuckled as he put the last welds on the current coupling. "That's done. Ready to release."

"Roger. Releasing. They're not pirates," Rae said, as she released it—slowly, to be sure it held. Together, they moved to the next spot, and she grabbed the tether to pull the next one to her. As she stuck it in place, she continued. "Their ship is too small, even for an indie op. They would not be armed with projectile weapons. And what was with those clothes? Coupling in place. Ready to weld."

"Ready to weld, copy. Starting first contact point now. They did look like something out of a movie," he admitted. "You know, you have a real talent for this."

"Welding? You're doing the work."

"No! Handling emergencies. You kept a cool head—"

"Ha!"

"Second contact point welding now. Oh, you snapped a little, but you didn't belittle anyone. You kept everyone calm and focused. You listened to ideas and had some great ones, yourself—like this. I'm just saying you're underutilized as a pilot, even a pilot at a major company. Plus, I heard you praying under your breath. You've got faith, even under pressure. Moving to the other side."

"Other side, copy." She shifted her gloves to give him access. "You're not trying to recruit me, are you, Father?"

"What if I am?"

"I'm not exactly Sister material! I'm rough and cranky—"

"—and you cornered a priest on his way to a connection to ask him for a Sacrament. You'd be surprised how many Rescue Sisters start out as rough, cranky, adrenaline junkies. Think about it. Pray about it."

She wanted to laugh—the idea was too ridiculous!—but she felt a funny little shiver inside. *Maybe...*

Nah.

Maybe?

"Rae? I said this weld's complete. Ready to move to the other side."

"Oh! Copy. Moving to the other side."

As he finished the welds that attached the other part of the coupling to *Lucky Charms*, he asked, "Think that will get us to Ceres?"

"Unless the panels decide to rip off," she replied sardonically.

But he answered with playful seriousness, "So, fifty-fifty?"

The rest of the trip went surprisingly well. The panels held as Rae nursed them to cruising speed, and with everything but basic life support off, there wasn't much on *Lucky Charms* to break and cause trouble. Father worried about their prisoners, but when he used the wristcomp Stormy had stolen to contact them, he received vile threats and profanities. Obviously, they were not in great shape, but good enough.

"I could hear the turkeys in the background, but they didn't seem to be attacking any longer. I guess the lack of gravity has them disoriented—or they're sleeping it off," Father said.

Their passengers, too, had decided to sleep off the last of their intoxication. It made for a quiet trip back. Rae tried to think and pray about Father's outlandish suggestion, but mostly she kept coming back to how she was going to report this whole fiasco to the Company.

Plus, texts showed up on the stolen wrist-comp: *Status? Did you get them? ETA? And I swear, if you double-cross me!*

Obviously, someone on the inside had known about her valuable cargo and had planned the hijacking. They may have even meant for the bomb wreck the ship first and then the "pirates" to swoop in and take the cargo. But *Lucky Charms* had broken down first, throwing their plans out of whack.

Suddenly, she smirked. *I disrupted a ring of thieves within the Company. I captured their ship and the thieves—and the cargo and passengers are intact. Mostly. Certainly enough to get paid for. I'm a fracking hero! They gotta give me a bonus for this. Right?*

She was feeling pretty good, and even better when she saw the moon-like asteroid Ceres and the station called.

"This is Ceres control space to unidentified craft. State your ID and purpose."

"Ceres! You are a sight for sore eyes! This is Captain Rae Marie Martingale, piloting *Lucky Charms*—or at least I would be. We were attacked by marauders, but we overpowered them. *Lucky* is not operational, so we took over the *PINA* and have *Lucky* in tow. Request a landing vector and a tug—she's not the most maneuverable in this state."

"Uh… the *Pina*?"

"*Pirate In Name Only*. Can I get a vector?"

"Standby. *PINA*, what's your cargo?"

She thought a moment. "Freefall pickled turkey and salty pirates."

"Excuse me?" The controller lost all pretense of professionalism.

She sighed. "It's been a long day, Control. Please have live animal wranglers, the station police, and the port authority ready to meet us.

"What?" Rae shouted. It seemed like that was the motto of this mission. She was tempted to create a mission patch with a turkey and that one word just to commemorate the experience. "I stopped my ship from getting hijacked, uncovered a plot within the company—I even brought back the ship that tried to rob us!"

She was in the Company comptroller's office on Ceres port, still in her scat-stained uniform, her hair finger-brushed and greasy, her stomach growling, and her heart hammering at the bill the Company had just presented to her. It was two years' salary!

The Company manager looked genuinely sympathetic but not concerned enough to do anything about it. "And the Company appreciates your hard work. However, you confiscated a passenger's property without prior authorization, released, then inebriated, valuable livestock, and caused damage to the ship."

She slapped the tablet on his desk--gently, lest she break it and get billed for that, too. "This is ridiculous! First off, I'm allowed to divest unruly passengers of potential weapons—"

"It was a flask." He sneered patronizingly.

"It was Three-oh-Seven Ale."

"Oh. Well, still—"

"The drunken passengers released the turkeys—"

He held up his hand to stop what would have been a satisfying tirade. "The decision has been made. Please report to Accounting to discuss a payback schedule."

He handed her the tablet and waved his hand in dismissal, but all she could do was stare at the number. She wouldn't be able to repay in a decade, even after giving them everything she'd saved up.

She wanted to fling it at his head. She wanted to scream. Instead, she stood there panting and blinking against the tears that threatened to spill over. I'm trusting. I'm trusting. I'm trusting.

She barely registered the polite knock on the manager's door.

"Excuse me," a cultured voice broke into her prayers. "Are you Rae Marie Martingale, pilot of *Lucky Charms*?"

God, what now? You are really pushing it. She scrubbed her eyes, then turned around. "Yes?"

The man, tall and slender, with a posture to go with the accent, blinked. Drat! She must look as upset as she felt.

"Sorry," she muttered. "Bad day. Can I help you?"

He cleared his throat. "I'm sure, after all that happened on your voyage here. Completely understandable. My employer requests an audience."

The manager stood. "Miss Martingale has already been punished for her actions."

She opened her mouth to protest, but confusion held her back. Was he defending her or covering the Company's butt?

The man looked down his nose at the manager as if he were an absurd little cog. "Her deeds have been nothing but exemplary."

Then he turned to her. "Miss Martingale, my employer, Augustus Cole, would like to offer you a job piloting for ColeCorp."

"Wait—Cole? He's the egoist billionaire who wanted live turkeys for his dinner?" She was so shocked, she didn't even feel embarrassed by her words.

The man replied with aplomb. "The very one. If you'll accompany me to the *Stellar Opalescence*—"

The manager cleared his throat. "Excuse me, but Miss Martingale owes the Company a great deal of money..."

His bravado wilted under the too-polite stare of Cole's man. "I...have an itemized list," he concluded lamely.

"I'll be most interested to see it."

She barely heard them. Could this be it? Her way out at last? Would Cole buy her out? She'd gladly be an indentured servant if it meant flying for ColeCorp.

And yet... That suggestion Father had made nagged at her. Hanging out with other cranky adrenaline junkies and getting to attend regular Mass?

I'm young. I can be patient, she told herself as she followed Cole's man—he still hadn't given her his name—out of the office and to a waiting car. He held the door for her, took a seat opposite her, and spoke his destination to the AI driver. They rode in silence; he, looking over something on his screen that apparently he found distasteful. Or maybe it was just her. She had gone straight from securing the *Lucky Charms* to the manager's office: chasing turkeys, fighting pirates—not to mention, EVA repairs—all had left her a little ripe, even by space hauler standards.

"Maybe I should clean up first," she ventured.

"Accommodations will be provided," he assured her.

The car slowed as it arrived at the private berth for the *Stellar Opalescence*. Rae gaped out the window at the ship. That was no ship. It was a flying art! Not just the design, which was somehow sleek enough for atmosphere, but the way the skin glowed with designs. Was it reacting to the natural radiation of space? She'd heard of such technology, but to see it--

If the controls are half as responsive as the ship is beautiful...

It had not one, but three airlocks. They passed the one for cargo, then the one for passengers, then stopped at a smaller airlock that led, she assumed, to the crew quarters. With a nod to the security guards at the lock, they went through and emerged in a narrow hallway with doors on either side. She barely had time to take in the carpeting and—were the walls painted?—when Cole's man ushered her into a small stateroom.

He pointed past the narrow bed to an alcove. "Showering facilities are in there. A female employee shall be here presently with more suitable attire."

"Thank you," she said cautiously, "but how much will this cost me?"

He gave her a ghost of a grin. "For the duration, you may consider yourself a guest of Mister Cole." With a short bow, he left without telling her the duration of what.

With a shrug, she went to the alcove, grasped the handle, and turned it on. Hot water sprayed from an opening at the top. She squealed with joy. An actual water shower!

She washed herself twice just to enjoy the feeling of the lather, and when she emerged, wrapped in a thick robe that had been hanging on the back of the door, she found not one, but two women waiting for her. One had a bag with brushes and other beauty implements, while the other was gripping a rack from which hung several beautiful outfits. The one with the bag introduced herself as Lilly from the Salon, and the other was Starlina from the Boutique.

"We're here to prepare you to meet Mister Cole," one said cheerily, while the other pulled one of the dresses—no, the gowns—off the rack and held it for her approval.

"Uh," Rae hesitated. "I think there's been some misunderstanding. Maybe you have the wrong person?"

"Miss Rae Marie Martingale." It was not a question but a statement of proof.

"Yes, but…" She opened and closed her mouth like a faulty valve, then finally blurted. "Just exactly does Cole expect from me?"

The two blinked at her; then comprehension set in, and they laughed.

Starlina started, "Oh! No, not that! It's just that, well, this is a luxury liner—"

"There are standards!" the Lilly cut in.

"And your uniform, even if it were clean!" Starlina emphasized her point with a shudder.

"We're burning it," Lilly concluded.

"Okay," Rae said slowly, "but shouldn't I have a uniform instead?"

They looked at her like she was mad. "But he hasn't hired you yet."

Rae did not feel especially reassured, but it was let them help or meet Cole in wet hair and a bathrobe. The girls were surprisingly accommodating. Lilly used her talents and her products to bring out Rae's natural curls, while Starfire offered a simple but probably insanely expensive tunic with long, tight sleeves and a tail that came mid-calf, with matching tights. It looked elegant without being extravagant, and it worked with her mag boots, which someone had taken and polished while she was in the shower. She had to admit, she felt very much like Cinderella, especially when they led her to a huge room with chandeliers, a dance floor, and row upon row of white-tablecloth-draped tables.

Or maybe Space Hauler Barbie. She paused at the door, suddenly confused and shy.

"I thought I was being interviewed," she protested, but her escort was gone.

Was this part of the process? Did she have to prove she could mingle with the rich and leisurely without making a fool of herself? There were six utensils at each plate! She'd only ever used a knife and a spork. She may as well head back to the Company now. Maybe they'd let her keep the outfit, and she could sell it to pay off part of the debt?

"Rae!" the familiar voice of Father Kyle sounded from across the room, and the priest excused himself from the people he was speaking to and went to her. "You look fantastic. How are you feeling?"

"Confused," she said as she took his proffered elbow. He led her past the mingling groups, who for the most part ignored them in favor of their own conversations. "This butler guy—"

"Macon?"

"Maybe? He never told me his name. Anyway, he finds me at the Company offices and whisks me away here, where I'm pampered and coiffed, and I thought Cole wanted to hire me or something—"

"But I do!" said a tall, blond man. He closed the distance between them and took her hand. "Augustus Cole, at your service. Enchanté." He kissed her hand.

"You're—"

"The egoist billionaire who wanted fresh turkeys for Thanksgiving dinner. And you are the intrepid pilot who protected my cargo from damaged equipment, drunks, and even pirates!"

"They weren't exactly pirates..." she demurred.

"How did you know?" he asked.

"Other than they were dressed like something out of a movie? The shoes. No pirate would board a ship without mag boots. They never take gravity for granted like stationsiders do."

"Told you she was smart," Father said.

Rae blinked at the priest. "You two know each other?"

Cole shrugged. "He's heard my confession a time or three. He was supposed to have taken the shuttle I'd sent to Waylaid for him, but he insisted on meeting me at Ceres instead. Said he felt 'called to scout.'"

"Really?" Rae gave him a suspicious look, which he met with an innocent smile.

"Well," Cole said, now taking her arm from Father Kyle and leading her to a table. Others caught sight of him and starting taking their seats as well. "I'm so very glad he did, because I would never have learned what an incredible captain you are. Your talents are wasted with that ridiculous shipping company, and I cannot abide waste."

Cole had brought her to the head table, which was already occupied by several people—most notably, the captain of the *Stellar Opalescence*. Cole made quick introductions, then clicked on his glass. By some unspoken convention Rae had never heard of, the room went silent.

Cole asked Father to say grace, then he himself said a few words about fellowship and humankind's grand destiny to the stars, blahblahblah. Rae, still reeling from the change in her station, only registered part of it. What was she doing there?

Then she heard her name.

"—is a prime example of that entrepreneurial spirit. Orphaned daughter of an independent trader, she has let neither misfortune nor lack of educational opportunities get in the way of what she wanted. Instead, she augmented her skill and talent with practical work—"

She cringed. Was that why she was there? To be some kind of showcase? Cause du jour?

Father nudged her with his elbow, so she held her tongue and nodded as people toasted her as the Savior of Thanksgiving Dinner. She made a mental note to correct Cole on the details of her life story later.

"Now," Cole said, smiling at her while the waiter set a large, covered platter on the table. With a flourish, he pulled off the cover to reveal a roast turkey. The table clapped, Rae with them.

As Cole carved, he continued talking to Rae as if he'd not been interrupted. "Tell me: Every hero deserves a reward. Your passengers have been handsomely compensated, enough to make their wives forgive any drunken revelries. Young Jaques is being apprenticed to a mining demolitions team on one of my asteroids. Father, of course, asked no reward, although I think the convent on Minerva is due a new shuttle. So that leaves you. What do you want?"

He placed a slice of breast meat on her plate.

"To fly your ship!" she said, making the captain snort. She corrected herself, "I mean, any of your ships. If we could work out a contract—"

Father grinned, but it was obvious he was disappointed. He looked down at his own plate. "So, you've decided, then?"

She felt awful. "No, I have. I thought about it. Prayed, even—as much as I could while dealing with everything. I'm sorry, Father. The Company's charging me damages for the trip. I can't join the Rescue Sisters until I pay that off."

Suddenly, Cole started laughing. "Really? That's what you want? To join the Order of Our Lady of the Rescue?"

"Yeah!" she flared. "What's wrong with that?"

"Absolutely nothing! We need more Rescue Sisters in the system. But why didn't you ask for that in the first place? Never mind—consider your debt paid. Really, there won't be any charges anyway, once my people have acquired the company. Imagine—trusting my turkeys to that rustbucket!"

"That's what I said!" Rae exclaimed.

"Well, then, Miss Martingale, consider yourself free to follow your Calling. And Father—looks like I owe the Order another shuttle."

It took a moment for the meaning of that statement to be clear in Rae's mind. She turned to Father Kyle. "Did you bet I was going to join up?"

He shrugged and picked up his fork. He bit into the turkey and chewed. "I had a good feeling about you when I heard your confession," he said after swallowing.

"Huh." She tucked into her own meal. She thought she could taste a hint of 307. Or maybe it was just the memories. Still.

It seemed that sometimes God did call on a bad day.

Keep in Touch

If you want to learn about future books, please

- Sign up for my newsletter. https://fabianspace.substack.com/subscribe more short stories, updates and a free book!
- Visit my website at https://karinafabian.com
- Follow me on Facebook: https://www.facebook.com/Karina-Fabian-Speculative-Fiction-with-a-Grin-2233839790277963

There's More Fun in FabianSpace!

Science Fiction

Space Traipse: Hold My Beer: Redneck ingenuity and common sense in a Star Trek-ish universe. Enjoy the adventures of the *HMB Impulsive*.

The Rescue Sisters: Intrepid women doing dangerous missions in space for the love of God and humankind.

The Old Man and the Void: Dex hunts relics on the edge of the black hole, and bags the catch of a lifetime.

Jovian Heat: As the next Great Storm of Jupiter rises, Cass must find the father of a baby in peril—but the father died before the child was conceived.

Fantasy

DragonEye Story: Vern's a snarky dragon on the wrong side of the Interdimensional Gap, solving crimes, battling evil, and saving the universes on an all-too-regular basis.

Madness of Kanaan: Deryl isn't crazy; he's psychic, and aliens of two worlds thinks he can save them. Maybe he can—but can he regain his sanity in the process?

Horror

Neeta Lyffe, Zombie Exterminator: Neeta's an average exterminator, taking out bugs, rodents, and the undead. Can she keep her friends alive, pay her bills, and find romance?

Frightliner and Other Tales of the Supernatural (with Colleen Drippé): Truck-driving vampires terrorizing the road, Southern women doing what needs doing, a zombie wedding—a great story collection for horror lovers.

About the Rescue Sisters

The order started on the L5 station, which is on the LaGrange trailing the moon. Gillian (Later St. Gillian of L5) was the wife of the inventor of artificial gravity. Ironically, he was so severely injured in an accident with his machine that he could no longer manage in Earth's gravity, so she left Earth to join him on L5. After his death, she took holy vows and petitioned to start an order of religious sisters in outer space.

While they do many things, Gillian chose search and rescue for the mission because it was a high-demand, high-risk operation that commanded high prices. By doing the work for "air, supplies and the love of God," they paved the way for their religious order to grow.

Skirts would be inconvenient and potentially embarrassing if the artificial gravity cut out, so Gillian chose wide-legged pants and a simple T-shirt under the skinsuit. The practical habit caused some scandal but was eventually accepted on stations and low-gravity environments, and grudgingly allowed "dirtside."

Under Gillian's leadership, the order grew to several locations, including L5 and Phobos, where there's a training convent. When she died, spacers claimed to have seen her apparition and credited her with saving them from accidents or other perils. Many of these miracles were confirmed and she was sainted.

We have several other stories with these sisters, which I'm going to start publishing.

Acknowledgements

This is a story I've wanted to write for ages. I got the idea from the filk song, "An Asteroid Named Rest Stop" by Julia Ecklar. (In fact, it's the second story inspired by filk songs.) I loved the thought of a pilot having such a bad day it makes her want to become a religious sister. I started the story at least a decade ago, but didn't know where I wanted to take it. Sometimes, a story just needs to sit.

I'd like to especially thank the Catholic Writers Guild SFF Crit group for all their wonderful comments, especially their encouragement to portray the Mass less "in terms of any joy, or any emotional reward for it, but the terrible necessity of it." (as Mark Baker eloquently put it.) Or as Rena said, "This should be Mass with toddlers."

Thanks, Rena Shannon, G.M. Baker, Matthew Schmidt, and Marie Keiser.

Finally, thank you, reader, for joining me on these adventures. Please leave a review, and don't forget to check out Discovery!